I0743415

Over the Fact

BY K. LEE

Over The Fact

Published by Krystal Lee Enterprises (KLE Publishing)

Please send comments and questions:

Krystal Lee Enterprises
www.KLEPub.com   AuthorKLee.com
770-240-0089 Ext. 1

Printed in the United States of America.

ISBN: 978-1-945066-07-8

Book Production: KLE
Cover Design: KLE: Krystal Lee

I pay tribute to my Lord and Savior Yahshua the Christ, and I acknowledge The Most High in all that I do!

This book is written to inspire those who have been lied to and only told facts that bend our thoughts so that we conform to believe lies. Shame on those who have benefited from lying to the Lord's chosen, and may the Lord be their judge and the vindicator of us who have lost too much believing a lie and then teaching those lies to our children for it to continue generation to generation. The lies cease now, today, and may TRUTH pour out from this book.

Special thanks to my family for always encouraging, protecting, and desiring me to fulfill my purpose against all odds. My beautiful mother, Ms. Yulanda and Ms. Joan, thank you for constantly lifting me up in prayer. To my children, who always remind me to lead even when I am tired of being an example! Of course, I acknowledge my sister, T.C. Martin, who reminds me family is beyond blood. My family, friends, and readers, without you, where would I be? Love you all, always.

Table of Contents

Lies Over the Fact!

Lies are typically told to uphold people, companies, or governments, images, personas, and ideas. If this were a case to be solved by a detective, they would look at the motive associated with a crime. What provoked this person to want to rob a bank, harm, or even kill someone?

There are key ingredients that lead people to lie, steal, cheat, or even kill. The tipping of the scales that drive people mad are their emotions. When something gets under the skin, it can drive a person to see colors. Red, like a bull, pushes for the most intense resolve regardless of the unforeseen, but sometimes known, outcomes.

So, what has to happen in life to push a person to the breaking point? That is the quest of man's greatest adversity: Fallen Angels to receive the answer.

The world has been turning for centuries. Some would argue millions or billions of years. Man cannot agree, but what is sure is that people and their desires don't change that much over time.

If people are given a lie to weaponize their anger toward someone or something else, there is no telling what may happen in the close or distant future. So what are these hot issues, lies, that has man huffing and puffing at each other, over the fact, that they are not each other's enemy?

The fact remains that man's number one enemy is not the Most High, aka Yahweh, nor the people you see, but the enemy that has bewitched man by pushing hot buttons to trigger reactions. At this time, a hand likely would raise in a classroom, belonging to a person who would ask, "Excuse me, but what do you mean?" Lies are at the bedrock of any major complication.

Lies don't have to be spoken, they can be heard in the mind and believed as if those things were true. The fact they were never stated or spoken aloud, doesn't mean they are not in play. The biggest game the fallen angels play, the devil among them, is to convince people their thoughts are their own.

Inside a man's mind, inner thoughts exist, reasoning and bantering over ideas, truth, realities, facts, and lies. This internal dialogue says, "You can get away with that." Many would not commit a crime or tell a lie if they didn't believe they could get away with it. Somewhere, this false confidence exists that the person will be all right in the end. This assurance seems to cloud judgment, outweighing even the facts of life. In today's society, that proof can be overlooked for the false pretense of innocence, but the Almighty, who overlooks the earth, would always be the judge.

He sits on His high thrown and looks down to earth. There is nothing done under the sun that slips past His surveillance. He sees all and knows all, confessed and hidden. Can one truly get away with anything with a being so GRAND overlooking the earth? Can even the fallen angels slip past His sovereignty?

So what makes man believe, for an instant or a lifetime, they can dodge a punishment that the Father deems fair treatment? The funny saying, "Hunting is no fun when the rabbit has the gun," has tickled and flirted with minds. Who wants to imagine a world where they are not in control or on top and rising fast?

Sinners and saints, neither wants to envision a life where they're under the feet of another. In fact, the first will be the last. The last will be first, and again, the first becomes first. The natural order that Elohim has established through His Word is until forever. No matter the plans and schemes of the enemy of Adonai, none can remove His authority from earth.

The whispers, "This person will take your wife." "That race or ethnic group will take your position in the world." "The Lord's chosen people aren't who we chose." "We chose to rewrite history with our spin, our success, our fate in our hands." But is this possible? Is man, demon, fallen angel, ghost, or principality able to force the Almighty's hand?

Can anyone deny His sovereignty? Able to tell Him "no" to what belongs to Him, and He bows down? Elohim never operates in reverse. He has many directions and planes He operates on, but one is not backward. Adonai will not back down but move past those denying Him. The Most High is so vast that He goes beyond the furthest distance man can see to set a trap to turn His children back to Him.

Adonai can impact the past by arranging the future. He is not subject to time nor is He bound by lies. History is often believed to be made up of "his story." Another common saying, "A happening can be told in three ways: his way, her way, and then the truth." The Word is the Truth.

Lies are a weight around a person's, government's, company's, and even country's neck. When a lie is told, another, and another, has to be lodged in to uphold the first lie. The more splints added to support a wooden beam, the more likely it will give way to the weight up above it. The truth beats down on lies. Aside from what may be the current facts, the established truth will have its way.

Truth Over the Fact!

The Truth belongs to the Lord and His chosen. A reprobated mind Adonai can permit for every man. He had King Nebuchadnezzar lose his mind, eat grass, and roam the ground like a cow. He gave that king over to insanity and only brought him back when and because He elected to do so.

No one or anything can box Him or pluck out of His hand what belongs. A lie must be established in a person's heart and mind for them to receive and operate from it. Many have accepted lies, unaware that's what it is because they disguise it as "their truth." There is only one truth, one faith, and one baptism.

So these lies give men charge, pump them up, or deflate them. Unaware, the believer is robbed of protection from the very one deceiving them. When people, Holy children, walk out of the hands of

Adonai, they are living at their own risk!

Some may say, "If Yahweh made a man eat grass and allowed His people to enter into slavery, perhaps no one should serve Him." That is what emotions, suckered by a lie, would think and believe. To convince those who will be beguiled into thinking The Almighty is evil, not man's emotions or the fallen angels' deceptions.

The fact is, The Creator entrusted man with Earth after He removed the assignment from Lucifer. Lucifer was the guardian of Earth. He was entrusted to protect this planet like a king would ask a knight or a president with generals beneath his umbrella. At no point did the Lord have to ask Lucifer for permission to remove his assignment. Nor did He have to clear it with him or anyone else that He chose to put man here and give them dominion.

The Truth is that fallen angels hate everything about man because trying to be like humans costs them everything. Fallen angels cannot ever get into the presence of the Most High. They know what it's like to turn their back on the Father of Life because they did it themselves. They know the loneliness, darkness, sadness, and pain.

The enemies of Yahweh want to hurt Him by entrapping His children to believe their lies. So they watch: What makes man happy? If we manipulate them with what pleases them, what could we use to trap them? If a person likes food, how can we change that from giving them life to bringing death?

If people like to love and share that love through sex, how can the fallen warp their understanding? The enemy thinks about how they can undo what the Lord has done, only not do it with their hands but in man's mind. If they can get believers to deny the truth for a lie, they got man pinned between a rock and a hard place.

These emotions fallen angels have against man are because they fell out with the Most High. They want to share their poison with any man should they accept their lies as truth. At some point, man should stop and say, "Does lying even prevent the inevitable or simply delay the timing?" Over the fact that events take time, know the truth, Elohim is still in control and time only passes because He says so. It is not man cheating his destiny or delaying the timing; it is simply man living out his course in the big picture.

The Father created Time. He is under Adonai's feet. Just like the devil fell from being second in charge but didn't lose his gift of music. Time also fell from dwelling among The Father and didn't lose his gift of time.

These fallen angels brought their talents down to share with man. They intend on teaching their talents to those who would listen, only not for their benefit but to kill off each other. At first, they thought to rule, but their bodies were taken when The Almighty killed their flesh. If legions can get believers to turn on themselves and people outwardly, they do the work of the enemy. They are essentially conquered by the fallen because they were blinded by lies to accept the truth.

Yahweh never made hell for man. He made it as a cell to hold all the fallen angels and their offspring.

Some people today say, "Hell is my home." "I deserve hell for all I have done wrong," or "I will gladly go to hell to do this or that." What is man saying or agreeing to? Why are they laying their lives down with the fallen if the Lord doesn't require it?

Christ has already laid His life down in exchange for any and all wrongs committed by holy children. So why are they still willing to die, not even in the place of demons but with them? People living wrong doesn't change the location of demons or the devil. When a believer lives right, the heavens rejoice, and when wrong, hell only holds their spot if they are not in the Book of Life.

The big picture is the Father of Lights wins. He made the oath that every work He starts, He finishes. He has never fought a battle He could not win, and that is why it pains Him to see His people perish. Knowledge of the truth, believing and operating by it, sets believers free! What if someone has the truth but doesn't believe it?

Belief Over the Fact!

There is no doubt that what a person believes can carry them a long way. This path can take someone towards his or her betterment or into a sunken place. Simply meaning, life events that take a person further into depression or anger. These people usually feel there is one sting after the next because they likely hit the hornet's nest.

In life, everyone must choose what he or she believes. Some may say, "I believe in nothing." Sure, everyone believes in something, even if they cannot define it. People believe that as they drive here or there, they will make it. Having a positive or pessimistic view of life is also a demonstration of belief.

Watching the news, or simply having friends,

one would hear of many who didn't arrive at their destination, but this fact doesn't stop anyone from hopping into a car and driving all the same. What can be derived from this simplistic example. Over the fact everyone has different experiences, thoughts, and viewpoints, there are beliefs established in people's minds that direct their life's direction.

If people believe all things are possible, they are neither fearful nor deterred from accomplishing goals when life throws curveballs. This fearlessness Adonai wants to give as freedom to His children. When an individual knows they have backup, acting like a superhero is understandable. No one is going to attack a group or the world if they have backup from the one Who is necessary to sustain the dream.

A needed associate to belief is hope! Hope will have a person believe that, over all the facts, something is possible. The Lord is the creator of HOPE! He provides a great escape in the most seemingly daunting circumstances. Some may think, "How can we clean up a mess that appears to be in every sector of their life?" "It's problems in the schools, church, inside my home, heck, even within me!"

Where can healing begin if we are stuck on a wheel, running without direction, and helpless to jump off the wheel and escape the cage? Something has to happen to set us free. Reminding the chosen they are not slaves. They are off the wheel and no longer caged.

When first trained, the elephant has to be conditioned to accept captivity. They were born free, even if they were in a zoo. Babies don't have leashes around their necks. Some even play with humans, but when they are awakened and realize the limits attempting to be set upon their lives, it should be no shock if there is some pushback.

Some would get mad at the baby elephants for wanting their freedom when the zookeeper has been so kind to them. They gave them everything they seemingly needed to survive, yet they wanted more—the elephant wanted freedom. Is this not how men think of people they believe are inferior?

No one can look and say people are people when, first, individuals don't truly feel that way. Some believe people are dispensable, property, bodies, human capital, or are breathing things that look similar but don't hold the value. War is evidence of how man feels about each other. Many are okay with killing their enemy about an object, resource, or information they have that another covets.

People come up with pretty lies to sell the belief that killing this person to protect people from a possibility is justified. We must war on terrorism, race, governmental politics, etc. What about the real war?

If someone can control how a person thinks about themselves, they no longer have to chain them or cage them, they are already conditioned for captivity. Many believe they are free because they don't see jail bars, they have escaped the physical cell, but their hearts, minds, and souls are trapped and starving for truth!

Before anyone can take back something that was stolen, they have to know they have been robbed. How can a person know if they have been robbed? They need to take inventory. The Bible says to examine oneself to see if she or he is in the faith. Likewise, people must look at what they believe and choose to see what is over the current facts.

Most facts result from a series of events that lead to that given destination. No fact simply popped up. Often, facts are created by decisions. Man can make a decision that will generate facts. If a person chooses to tell a lie, the truth still is, but the decisions people make after hearing the lie create facts. Regardless of who believes it, even choosing not to believe becomes the starting fact for what happens next.

If black people hear, they are the Hebrew people of the Bible. Each person must decide if he or she believes it. Those who choose to consider it would likely do research. The fact is, what a person cares about—even in the slightest—they will do a quick Internet search at the least. If they find a possibility, a connection, they must choose to learn more or close the book.

For those that do not believe for one second they could be the people in the Bible, they may ignore what they heard and never look it up. Fact, belief doesn't change the truth, but it does change the facts. Both persons could in fact be Hebrews and have the blessings or the cursing listed in Deuteronomy. The one who studies would learn something about themselves, while the one who doesn't, likely lives life blind.

The fact is they both could be set free by knowing their history, ancestry, and their Elohim, but one will live life bound and the other free. Over the fact that the Most High gave His Son, the Word, so that His children may live an abundant life. Many of them have no belief. If there is but a small amount of belief, equal to a mustard seed, what a great thing Yahweh can do for His people and the world over!

Love Over the Fact!

The love and compassion Elohim has for His children pleased Him to sacrifice His Son to cover a multitude of sins. The death of Yahshua would be in vain if His people did not understand and believe that love was demonstrated on the cross. He is The Love that went into hell, took the keys of death, hell, and the grave to return to the Right Hand of The Father.

Christ suffered so that all of Adonai's children could live more abundantly. He removed the sting that death once had over believers and gave us eternal rest. As for believers, they are not tormented when they leave this realm but simply await their rebirth in their new heavenly body. Believers will be restored to what man was intended to be before the fall.

The closeness Adam and Eve had with the Most

High, His Word, and Presence has not been felt by anybody else since we got the boot. They were able to see into the heavens with their natural eyes wide open. The Creator of the Universe walked among them in the cool of the day and now we cannot see His face.

They were free to eat whatever they chose, and as long as they lived from every Word from the Most High, they maintained eternal life. Man today is now working, with the help of Christ and the Holy Spirit, to get back to where they began. The Lord promises to complete a work He starts. In the Hebrew tradition, it is a blessing to be born and laid to rest in relatively the same time period. It is as if the person lived a complete life to end where they began. The only difference is the growth one has experienced throughout life before they died.

Adam and Eve took for granted the love they received freely and openly from Yahweh. They didn't know how much it meant to feel as if the sun followed them. The earth produced fruit not because they worked or asked for it but as a provision from the Most High for His coveted creation.

The devil hates that the Almighty created something he felt should not inherit the gifts He gave. The devil and the fallen angels are green with envy, red with hatred, and blue from being choked out by the Lord and removed from this earth in the natural state as before.

The demons have an eternal headquarters in hell, reduced to a vapor, not even a shadow of their former selves. The devil is doomed to squirm around on his belly like a snake when he used to be the most beautiful angel. These once angelic beings have been put under any man's feet, and so they work in unison to capture the Lord's children, subjecting them to their harsh treatment.

The love that the Lord has determined to share with man, over the fact that they created the separation, demonstrates how deep His love is for believers. He is able to overlook sins and filth, cleaning up peoples' lives and restoring them to better than before. He not only restores man, but He goes to the highest degree. He will restore man to never age, get sick, experience loss, or remember the things former in the new heaven and earth.

All those who choose to love Him in return will experience life as it was created for living. The new heaven and earth, New Jerusalem, will be a sight for any man to see. Yes, there will likely be gold, precious metals, stones, homes, and unusual travel, but most importantly, the Most High will be the ruler on earth through His Son, Yahshua the Christ, as King!

How sad it is for those who would have lived, died, and never experienced—or will, the Love that the Good Lord has for those who belong to Him. This eternal separation was not Adonai's plan for man but the fallen angels who disobeyed Him. Disobedience, man did not know until the devil taught it to them. Likewise, there are many things man learned from fallen angels that have continued to corrupt our nature.

The devil and demons attempt to paint their offerings and temptations as gifts, but they are mere flattery. They are insults, sins, hatred, fear, pain, delusions, perversion, abuse, deception, manipulation, curses, racism, homosexuality, narcissism, stealing, and killing wrapped up as gifts. Fallen angels do not have Love, so they cannot give what they don't have to someone else.

To expect anything helpful to come from an enemy is foolish, gullible, and out of touch with even reality. Those who hate the air man breathes are not capable of desiring the best life now for them but eternal destruction by any means necessary. The bigger the weapon, they say, "Great!"

The nastier the attitude, they repeat, "Great!" The more ruthless, selfish, self-hating, racist, murderous, lying, conniving man can become, the fallen angels shout to the heavens, "Great!"

The Bible was permitted by the Most High to show His love towards His children. Adonai is all-knowing and knows there will always be a group that won't serve Him but finds enjoyment in pleasing themselves. He is not appealing to this group, but the ones He saved, bought at a price, He mourns over. It is not the Lord's will that many, especially a child of His, live an eternity in hell. The Elohim of All Creation is so much BIGGER than Hell, the Grave, Problems, Hurt, Sickness, Disease, Suffering, and Pain—He is The Great I AM!

The Great I AM cannot be harmed with weapons of mass destruction or even hellish people doing things orchestrated by their father, but it bothers the Lord to see His children turn away from Him. To choose a life of sin and self-gratification when the Master of eternity is opening a door of peace, and His presence before them is a severe slap in the face, and He won't let it rest.

Hate Over the Fact!

Some might ask, "How can an all-loving God hate?" That's like asking, "How can a parent have rules for their children?" Rules exist to keep people from something, good or bad. A loving parent creates rules to safeguard their children; likewise, the Most High has done the same thing.

The Lord has rules because He loves His children and wants to see them have everything He designed for them. Dominion over earth, peace, love, joy, and to be in the Lord's presence for eternity is what He had in mind. Man changed the plan by eating from the forbidden tree, simply disobeying the Lord's command.

Adonai has made many requests from His people. He gave instructions on what not to eat, whom not to marry, and how to live this life. He makes no apology for giving His final say and His expectations. He implies in the Bible, "My ways are higher than yours, as are my thoughts." When man grumbles about the decisions the Lord makes, it doesn't change His opinion on the matter.

When the Lord told His children not to eat from this tree, and they did, He didn't say, "Well, maybe I should have let them eat from the tree of knowledge. Perhaps I was a bad Father not to give them free reign in the Garden." "Maybe they can handle making their own mistakes and living with the consequences."

News flash, they got the boot from the garden, and to this day, man is struggling to accept their punishment for the choices they made. It is not the Lord that sins, but the one who commits the act. It is not the Lord that is wrong to say anything, but it is wrong for a person to try and contaminate His Word.

How can anyone know what the Lord hates and why if the people called by His name do not demonstrate the benefits? There are benefits to honoring Adonai's commands. The Almighty hates sin, and He has nothing to do with it.

So, who can blame the Lord for turning His face from sin? The Lord says He would never leave nor forsake His children; it does not say He will permit any kind of behavior in His presence. The Father of Lights has the permission to turn out the light and not watch or surely participate in actions that violate His character.

Likewise, He will not force anyone to come to

Him or follow Him if they do not want to. Now, this same freedom the Most High gives man, He authorizes the same and more of a prerogative for Himself. The Lord chooses whom He will have mercy, and if at all. Everything He has made belongs under His sovereignty because He is the Master Creator.

No matter how hard man tries—or fallen angels too, they will never be greater than the Creator. To prove the Lord's dominance, He doesn't have to punish people in the way of creating an outcome. By simply allowing results to play out according to their nature, the outcomes will provide a teachable moment.

When the Lord gave the Ten Commandments, He did so to keep man from becoming his own enemy. To command not to steal, kill, covet, lie, cheat, use the Lord's name in vain, worship idols, or disobey authority (parents), but to love Him and put Him first is not unreasonable. However, and sadly so, some will disagree.

Every man has an internal beacon that goes off when hellish things happen. No one needs to be told murder is wrong. Stealing, coveting, and being jealous/envious of someone else's things is wrong. The Lord put the beacon in man's heart.

In addition to the Ten Commandments, there are also six things the Lord hates and seven that are an abomination, as recorded in Proverbs 6:16-19. The word writes that he Hates: a proud look, a lying tongue, hands that shed innocent blood, a heart that devise wicked imaginations, feet that are swift in running to mischief, a false witness (liar) that speaks lies, and he that makes discord among brethren.

Notice what is written among the seven things and what seems to be on repeat. The Lord hates those who are busy trying to be in everyone else's business and can't handle their own. People who go around corrupting what they don't understand because they can't control it. These same ones desire for people to despise themselves and plant a twisted interpretation of self-love.

The facts many like to present are of the Lord hating people, races, cultures, faces, sexual preferences, and alcoholics, but He really hates evil operating in high places. Oppression, racism, abuse, fear, hatred, manipulation, lying, stealing, killing, and preying on the weak and unknowing. Those who steal from the poor through contracts and laws will be addressed, and the false interpretation of those laws will be addressed.

Many may feel that the Father has become uninterested because they don't see Him operating swiftly. No, the Father is patient to fulfill in this lifetime and the next. No one who gives to Him will carry a balance, nor will He fail to collect what is His.

The Master never created hell because he hates man but because the Father hates sin. Sin is the ticket that buys you a place in hell. Sin, when it is fully grown, brings death. Every man has sinned and fallen short of the glory except the Messiah.

He is the only one who has lived a perfect life,

so sin to all men is real and impacts everyday lives. Many live a life full of sin because one offense sparked an explosion. People become lovers of themselves when they are neglected by those whom they love.

People choose alternative lifestyles when they feel the natural order doesn't pick them. Many were raped, molested, or violated, and the after-effect is they live out the best course of action to soothe their hurt. Sometimes, people rob Peter to pay Paul. What everyone needs to realize is that no matter if they pay Paul or Peter, they are still in debt!

When is man going to get into the position of freedom and stay there? The Lord can redeem anyone and change any lifestyle to be like His—if they are willing. The Lord doesn't ask anyone to give under compulsion, not even their heart or soul. Anyone who worships Him must do so in spirit and truth.

Death Over the Fact!

The Lord has told man the ending to sin is death! If anyone continues to sin, death is assured. It may not be today or tomorrow, but it will come. When people disobey a command, a reprimand is assured. The Lord's chosen people were not above the law of reaping and sowing. Whatever a man plants does, he will reap a result.

If a person sows discord among brothers, the outcome will likely be dysfunction, lack of communication, hatred, and death—death of a relationship, freedom to love, or physical freedom. Cain did not learn from Adonai to murder; he did the act of his own free will. Likewise, the punishment for killing Able cursed his entire bloodline because the curse started with Cain and descended through his blood to whomever else.

This is basic science, like a disease that is passed on because of heredity. Man is guilty because the disease of sin flows through every man's blood. Sin and its impact can be felt throughout the legacy of man because of the First Adam and Eve.

For example, in the book Deuteronomy, chapter 28:15-68, Moses records the curses because of disobedience. Sin has to mature, which means time has to take place. A baby doesn't grow up overnight but matures over the years; whatever was at the foundation supports how they live their life.

So, what are the curses that man can see today because of disobedience? How many feel as if they spend a great majority of their time working, gathering for someone else to go on vacation? As the employee, you are doing the work but not benefiting.

I know when I think of countries, and for that matter a continent, there is a lot of agriculture hard work going on, but very little finances going to the people. In many of these same countries, we find that outsiders rule their government and language or dictate their culture. Do you see what I am seeing?

It's like a locust is consuming your harvest, and nothing you plant can thrive. Verse 38 talks about carrying much seed out and yet gathering very little. So many have sent out their talents into the world, but others put their name on their gifts, and the praise is not set aside for them but is stolen.

Death to favor for the Lord's chosen is demonstrated in Deuteronomy 28. The Father's pleasure in seeing His children blessed in the city and field with their comings and goings is canceled because they refused to worship and acknowledge Him. Amazingly, man believes they can handle an eternity without the Father when His chosen people couldn't manage a decade or a century without His presence.

The Truth belongs to The Lord and His chosen. A reprobated mind, Adonai can permit for every man. He had King Nebuchadnezzar lose his mind and eat grass. He roamed and grazed the ground like a cow. He gave that king over to insanity and only brought Him back when and because He elected.

The Messiah, said, "I lay my life down and will take it up again in three days" in John 10:18. He rose with the power to overcome death. In order for a believer, disciple of the Most High to live, that individual must first be born again. How can a person be born again? They must first die to sin.

In the natural state, man is dead in their trespasses. The Father of Lights does not listen to sinners (John 9:31). Further, He separates himself from sin as it builds up a barrier between the sinner and the Most High (Isaiah 59:2). So the sinner is a dead man in the eyes of the Father because He is the Life, the Truth (John 1:4).

An example of death that must not be set aside is the death of the Egyptians. The Father and He alone has the power to bring forth the Death Angel. He obeys the voice of the Father, and His Word is final.

The lamb's blood, a sacrificial lamb, had to be placed over the lamppost of the Hebrew households for the Death Angel to pass by. For those found lacking, the firstborns of that household were taken in one night.

The Father controls when a person is to die and for how long they will live from the Old Testament to the New, and from back then until the future. Death does not intimidate the Most High at all, and what may look dead in people's lives, countries, and nations, the Father is more than able to restore.

Can He make dead bones live? Can He bring life to a desert land? Can He pull a nation and peoples from a reprobated state in a twinkle of an eye? Can He un-prison a caged bird, people, nation, or continent?

Isaiah 28:8-9 says, "He will swallow up death forever. The Lord Yah will wipe away the tears from every face and remove the disgrace of His people from the whole earth. For the Lord has spoken, "And in that day it will be said our Yah; we have waited for Him, and He has saved us. This is the Lord for whom we have waited."

The fact man has breath, he appears to live. But if everything about them is dead, how can it be said they live? The Truth, a man or woman without the Father, absent of following His commands and hearing His voice, is dead in trespasses and sins (Ephesians 2:1 and 5).

Joy Over the Fact!

There is no secret that the Joy of the Lord is the strength of the believer (Nehemiah 8:10). Many may ask, "How can anyone have joy when it appears that so many odds, curses, people, police, nations, and other people hate you?"

If a person only finds joy when there is no rain, they will not truly understand what it means to be a disciple of the Most High. It rained on Christ. He had to go to the cross, be broken, and die, not because He caused the rain, but because it was the Father's will. It was for His glory!

No man can explain why Elohim does everything He does. Not even using the Bible can we dissect every thought the Father has. His way is simply above man's (Isaiah 55:9). The Creator is not a man, so His strength or ability cannot be halted. He is all-powerful and in control. He is the judge of everything, and no one is His ruler. He does not report to anyone or have to explain and give a reason for His choices. They are simply the Truth; His Word is Truth (John 17:17).

Christ had to find joy in what would appear to be a voided situation. He was going to be crushed so that others could be redeemed. He was being beaten for man's transgressions and every sin He took upon Himself at the cross.

The joy of many may be halted because there is a season for which things happen in life. A time to be glad and a time for sorrow. A time for planting and a time to harvest. A time to build up and a time to tear down.

This life cycle of ups and downs, as explained in Ecclesiastes, points to the toil in a man's and woman's life. Although it rains, that rain, for those who have the joy of the Lord, will function as restoration and hope that gives the believer a sense of peace in a world that offers none to many.

This joy that may appear unattainable when had brings comfort because those going through the rain know they are not doing it alone. The Word says in Hebrews 13:5, "He will never leave us nor forsake us." Even when His children have to reap what they sow and go through the storm, the rain, and dark times, still He is with us.

Joy is not defined by being happy with what

is going on, hence happening. It is about having un-shakable peace, joy, and the ability to praise the Father despite what is going on. It is an active choice to trust the supernatural power of the Most High instead of the facts.

The facts, many don't have much to be happy about some would claim. Health could be a factor, the loss of a relationship, witnessing a relationship die, drinking poisonous water, eating dead food (or genetically modified), being forced to make decisions, or having no choice because of your social or economic status. These are all reasons some would argue to be void of joy.

How can a person have joy with so much wrong in the world, their community, within families, even down to issues within oneself? The Father says anyone who isn't willing to lay their life down for Him does not deserve Him (Matthew 10:38). The Word says in John 14:27 that Christ, Yahshua, is the Prince of Peace. Peace is directly connected to Joy because peace resides where joy lives! If anyone lacks peace, by extension, they are lacking joy, which is the confidence that the Good Lord will take care no matter the facts, circumstances, or issues. His Word is greater.

The enemy comes to steal a believer's joy. John 16:22 says, "Therefore you now have sorrow, but I will see you again, and your heart will rejoice, and your joy no one will take from you." Yes, maintaining joy is a direct choice and one that has to be constantly re-enforced. Joy is also closely knitted to hope! Hope deferred can make a heart grow sick (Proverbs 13:12)! So health, wealth, and so much of your life are shaped by joy, hope, and believing in a better tomorrow, even if it evades your present.

Many of the works written by slaves and folks who have broken the mold and set a bar for people of color would point to their desire for their children to go higher. How many were deprived of an education, and now, today, every child can have an education in the United States regardless of race. Many blacks, arguably Hebrews, have privileges that were denied to their ancestors, but their children and children's children have the chance to do better.

We truly do stand on the shoulders of our ancestors and those who were willing to be the foundation for change. Every basketball player doesn't take the shot. Some are great at getting the ball down the court, others serve it up to the basket, while yet another slams it into the goal. Life is very similar. We share the load, share the joy, and find solace in knowing the Kingdom of the Most High is working through His children and going against all facts and social norms.

The joy they all have when a victory is won is not limited to the MVP. The power of joy is not limited to being felt by the last person who made the shot but by the entire team who contributed to the win. The entire body of Christ can celebrate the victory Yah is doing, utilizing His people in dynamic ways.

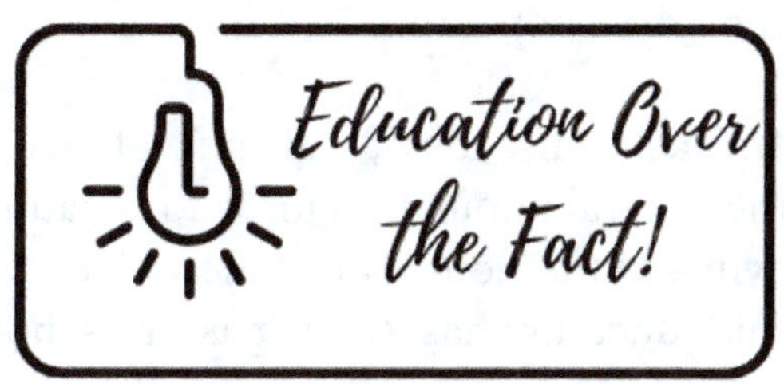

Education Over the Fact!

So what are the facts about education that the Word has said otherwise? Education would have many believe that their own history has no importance or place in their education. Many start their formal education during a time period in which their nation, culture, or societal norms were uprooted and changed by another governing body, social group, or government.

How can one truly know who they are or where they come from if their education has their beginning set in bondage? How can one get the truth if the facts would point to an inferior conclusion? How can your people have been the greatest architects, mathematicians, and worshippers if you are now the ones in bondage?

How can a conclusion be reached that a person has value if everything around them points to an opposite response? The business owners in urban areas do not look like the residents. The doctors and people in high esteem, as far as education and doing big business, typically don't share the same culture or social class as the urban population.

The facts, false ideas, and conceptions have shaped the general population for who is naturally smart, loving, kind, thoughtful, educated, lazy, and a threat. This education has leaked past the school. Entered the media and it projects images that are not true but hold as fact in many hearts.

From the time many can walk into the world, they hear the parallel of what it means to be black. No one seems to care to teach you your culture or imply you had a heritage before your ancestors came to the Americas. The only thing they can tell a person that has color is that you're black.

The only thing worse than no education is poor education. No education would humble a person to know they don't know everything. The poorly educated hold on to false truths and spit them to their children, continuing to spread the artificial facts. Women teach their children men of color are to be tolerated and not respected. You cannot hold a black man to the same principles as other men because they are not able to be faithful to one woman. They will be cheaters, and the woman has to accept that or get even.

Men are taught something similar. Women

are not fit to be trusted. Their loyalty is fleeting. Their hearts can be far off even though they perform the habitual habits to maintain a home. They are absorbed with fake hair, nails, eyelashes, and attire. These add-ons seem to be the only thing forthcoming about them. Due to shame, neglect, rejection, hurt, and pain, many women struggle to find their balance in life, and that sense of loss plays out in how they raise their children, both young women and man children.

This education, or lack thereof, should not be new information to the people it greatly impacts. Deuteronomy records this as one of many curses for disobedience on the people the Father had chosen. In chapters 28 and 29, the Bible records how the unraveling of many generations. They will be a reprobate with no one to turn them to their senses.

The woman who was once dainty and too high class to put her soles on the ground will now take from her children. She will eat the seed her children need. The young man, who was once regal and had dignity, power, and strength, has been brought to his knees by being displaced from his family.

He watches as another takes care of his children and dictates his reach and influence. He looks at his ex-girlfriend, boo, or could have been wifey as she moves on to the next, and his only prayer is for better days. Who wants another terrible man to raise their children as they helplessly look from afar?

Who would have ever chosen to have their children sold, their wives snatched away, abused, and harmed in front of their faces? How strong can you be if the best and strongest among you were turned against you, physically abused, humbled in the most horrible way, and their entire existence was forever questioned?

Sexual perversion and other unspeakable things befell these people. For the abused, they were rejected by their own because their child had a lighter complexion. Amongst those who looked like the abuser, that same mother was seen as nothing more than the help or free grazing property.

How can this education shape a people of culture and strong conviction? How can a people who had a language that lost it find it? How can this group fix the problem and reverse the curse that lingers over their families?

It begins with healing a relationship with the only one who holds the truth and is able to remove the curse, Yahweh.

Health Over the Fact!

The same chapters in Deuteronomy talks about how the health of Hebrews will be impacted by their living conditions. The blessings that were explained in the early verses, talks about being in good health and prospering. The curses remove that covering. Through changing diets, locations, and ingredients, even something as simple as water, has proven to impact brain function and spiritual connection.

Fluoride in the water is directly connected to reducing and blocking the connectivity of the penial gland. Many who have performed research on this gland find that it is substantially larger in melanated people compared to those with a deficiency. Not only does fluoride impact the spiritual makeup of special groups, but it also impacts the time frame of puberty for girls.

One can believe that fluoride has drastically sped up the onset of puberty in young women, reducing the time they have to enjoy their youth. Melatonin, a vital hormone that not only impacts puberty but also controls sleeping patterns and reduces free radicals in the body, has also been reduced. It is located near the pineal gland.

Why would teeth benefit supersede spiritual ones, your physical health, and your sleeping habits? It would appear a no-brainer to add fluoride to toothpaste only instead of tainting all drinking water in the name of saving teeth. Furthermore, why change the makeup, that is, the genetics of the food everyone eats, to be an artificial substitute?

Essentially, even live foods that could once fuel the body are now hindered because the seeds that give life are missing. The body is divinely created to self-heal, to purge food. When you fast, the body will naturally reset. If foreign radicals are in the body, the body reacts to control the situation.

The problem, if the body is not familiar with the ingredients or how to digest them, the body starts to break down. The way it was designed now doesn't function because the food you eat and the habits a person has take a toll on the body. Like the earth groans because of the sins of man, a person's body can start to give up because of poor habits.

Genetic splicing has already been implemented into food and it is now possible to control how the genetics in food impact a specific group down to sex, race, and ethnicity. It is a continued study and science for how the food pyramid was never designed to maintain the health of man, but perhaps to balance the health of financial sectors.

In urban areas, many are lactose and intolerant, yet WIC is heavily pushed in those same areas. Dairy is a known link to inflammation which is the contributing factor for any disease to take root in the body. Likewise, with adjustments in these products, soy milk and other substitutes still appear to have adverse effects. Soy milk contains estrogen a female growth hormone, it is not conclusive for how soy milk impacts people, but if it is not completely safe why sell it?

Soy milk can be a contributor to increased cancer specifically breast cancer, present thyroid issues, and feminize males drinking or using soy or using products such as tofu. Yogurts that include more than 23 grams of sugar are not healthy and present no genuine benefit. The probiotics in said yogurts have also been argued to not present any true health benefit either.

So if the milk, yogurt, and rice you are given, don't genuinely help, it would only appear a trap. Most rice on the market is filled with plastic, the cheese offered doesn't melt or burn, it too has plastic. If those offering help are simply exchanging one poison for another, is it really helpful?

Immunizations are also closely linked to long-term health issues in children, especially black males. It has been argued that autism has spiked some 30%, as recently reported in 2018. It is proposed that the link to this rise in autism cases is one in every 68 children compared to 1 in 88 just a handful of years before. Ironically, it is said the increase has no link to immunization.

This however is known, autism, is a combination of genetic and non-genetic, or environmental influences. What exactly is changing in genetics and how? What environmental changes are different now than before? Could it be global warming? Or is it likely cell towers, poisonous water, intolerable ingredients that fight with your diet, or the shots that inject possible foreign substances into the body?

These same shots are instructed by doctors and other pro-natural health advisors not to take. In addition, it has been proven that aborted fetuses are a known ingredient in immunizations. Why inject a dead baby into live humans? Then why inject that same substance into your soda beverages, foods, snacks, and other consumable goods? When companies asked why they use Semonyx in their products, it was said to be for flavor.

If this story held no foundation, which some argue, like Snoops.com and others, why would the state of Oklahoma present a bill in 2012 to ban the manufacturing of products containing aborted fetuses in their state, according to ABC News? The same article points to this finding about the same company, Semonyx, and they write, "Representative Shortey may be acting on claims that the San Diego-based company Semonyx used proteins derived from human embryonic kidney cells to test artificial sweeteners, NPR reported. The cell line, known as HEK 293, was created from a human embryo in 1970 and has become a staple in biochemistry labs around the world."

It's worth noting the fascinating story of Henrietta Lacks, a Hebrew woman whose DNA was utilized for pioneering medical research. Her cancer cells were taken without her knowledge, and she became the first immortalized human, contributing to significant advancements in science. However, it is unfortunate she did not receive any direct benefits for her critical contribution.

Using people of color to test drugs and watch the spread of diseases is not new to many people of color. The Tuskegee Experiment was conducted on black males, and a sum of 600 impoverished sharecroppers from Macon, Alabama, signed up. They were told by the United States Public Health Service they would get free government healthcare.

The important part they left out was that none of these men were sick. They intentionally injected them all with syphilis, and what was told to them to be a short 6-month study was truly a 40-year experiment. Of the 600, 399 of these men had latent symptoms of syphilis, and 201 were not impacted at all. Of those infected, this study kept going after the project's cancellation or defunding. The cure to the disease was in the hands of those conducting the experiment, but they chose to watch these men suffer and die instead.

The subjects were told they were being treated

for bad blood instead of being walking virus subjects. What is even more concerning about this project is that Tuskegee College is a historically black school that helped make this experiment possible. They, too, never got involved and turned a blind eye and ear to the deaths of these black men as well.

John Hopkins' poisoning experiment was conducted in 1993 on black children in Baltimore. The experiment is talked about in an article presented by Workers Vanguard, which says Ericka Grimes was a one-year-old who was intentionally exposed to high levels of lead paint. Ultimately, they had her living in a house with crumbling lead paint. The levels of lead increased triple fold in 5 months in her body. The damage was permanent brain damage, learning disabilities, and impaired hearing. She, too, was not treated, and the United States Government paid for the research.

In addition, this project was performed to see if slumlords could skip out on doing the necessary renovations for lead paint by band-aiding over the paint instead of removing it. I guess many black children had to become permanently ill in order to conclude that lead paint around children is wrong and now is illegal even in black neighborhoods. However, a close discussion with people living in urban neighborhoods would tell you that building codes are not enforced. Section 8 housing has black mold growing in project housing for minorities, and living conditions are far below standards.

Shame to say that in the 2000s, the battle with lead in the water in Flint has proven yet again that people in governing seats don't mind harming black children for convenience or experimental purposes. The fast food industry, which heavily targets urban areas, has also proven to have its interest at heart than the health of those that buy and eat their products. Whenever it is possible to buy a completed burger in a restaurant for $1, one must ask the question, "What am I eating?" Studies have been conducted and continue to be done on the meats sold in these restaurants.

Some claims may have no balance, but some likely do. Some of the facts passed down include that some meats contain traces of human flesh, horse flesh, cat, dog, rat, and other foreign ingredients. The McDonald's hamburger did not decompose. A scientist named Karen Haranhan kept a burger from 1996 to 2008 to prove these burgers do not decay; hence, the term "bionic burger" was created, and a museum, The Bionic Museum, was designed to support the science. Likewise, the 50 ingredients in most shakes created in these stores do not even contain milk!

How is it possible that meats can pass inspection and make their way into restaurant chains of every kind, and the public is not made aware of these claims on a large scale? How can something be called a milkshake if it has no milk? If health is directly related to wealth, is it a wonder why the gap is so wide between people of color and others? What has to puzzle many is how 201 subjects did not contract syphilis. Likewise, when AIDS was circulating, how was it that many were also immune to that virus, the flu, and many more diseases that continue to emerge? Is it a wonder why these black people, Hebrews, tend to self-medicate before they trust a doctor?

The Truth, the Lord said He would maintain a remnant. The Lord gave His word, and He gives new mercies every day to the many who need it. The science conducted on people of color is how scientists know as much as they know about developing fetuses, gynecology, surgery, and so much more. Many people were put through anguish and pain with objects created by those who wanted to dominate not only their work ethic but also their sexual preference.

Many from their youth are told to pray without ceasing. It is not foreign to have heard growing up, "Pray over your food. Pray over your family. No matter what it looks like, bless the name of the Lord!" These sayings were recorded in the Bible, but they were taught to many generations, and the power of prayer preserves and performs miracles even in the midst of challenging circumstances.

Life Over the Fact!

There would appear to be many reasons why death should be imminent. For many, time may be a shorter life span than others, but an important factor is to live a life worth living. Ancestors who stayed on the boat as they were dropped off in foreign lands, forced to work, and endured inhumane hardships must have said and believed greater was coming.

Even though many lived and died in chains, hope and belief in the Bread of Life kept them in times of sorrow. To live is sometimes more virtuous than to die. The Bible says blessed are they who follow His Voice, His commands, and are obedient to Him than those who sacrifice. In order for the world to move and fulfill the Good Lord's plan, He has a way of preserving His people by giving them the ability to endure until the curse is gone.

Four hundred years would appear a long time to live in hard conditions, but man says this not taking into account how their sins bothered the Most High. No man knows fully the penalties of sin except the simple solution: they lead to death. This life was not meant to be lived in any kind of way but was designed to work according to His will, especially for His children.

The Creator points to the children that are His and those that are of their father, the devil, the workers of evil (John 8:44). For His children, they are to acknowledge His ways and be a living sacrifice (Romans 12:1). How can a dead man or woman serve? Only if they passed doing the will of their father can they be an example of righteousness or evil.

Those who are the children of the Most High have access to knowledge, miracles, hope, and peace not available to others in the same situation. A common saying among saints is, "Favor ain't fair," and it isn't, but neither is this life. It is undeniable that there are guns pointed at some and not at others. Some will naturally be targeted, frisked, and searched because they will always fit the profile of another criminal.

Groups are marginalized not because they are trying to break the system but because they managed to wiggle their way out. Every time one succeeds, it appears that attempts to discourage and not encourage others seem to grow rapidly. A poem by Mya Angelou that catches the phrase perfectly, "Still I rise."

Although many plots, plans, diseases, conditioning, etc, have befallen this people group some feel they are as resilient as the cockroach and they manage to survive. To live despite the fiery darts of the enemy being shot above their heads and around them (Ephesians 6:16) takes Yah. There is no denying that this battle is not only a physical one but a spiritual battle for the people of Yah (God) to become and remain true.

Every day, people are given choices. What they do with those choices determines how they will live their life. It is believed that once a person becomes a believer, they are no longer their own man or woman, but they have made a committed decision to put The Father's ways above their own. They agree to count everything as dung. Things they have heard and were taught about themselves and the world around them are reduced to lower importance. They now allow the Word to recreate the True picture juxtaposed with the facts they have heard all their life.

This lifestyle believers are supposed to live is beyond a form of godliness that has no power to change and deliver, save, or redeem. The Bible says He is the living Word (1 John 2:24-25) and that He is the God of the living (Mark 12:27). Clearly, the Father is claiming that He is sovereign, but He is not the Father of lies (John 8:44), nor is He the Father of the workers of iniquity (Matthew 7:23), or the author of confusion (1 Corinthians 4:33).

So, the moment serving Him because confusing, one has to ask, who confused it? Why is His name the only name that did not remain the same if there is power in it? Yahweh and Yahshua are the names of

God and Jesus, but someone thought it a good idea to tamper with the Truth. The fact is that many today are being told and trained up to call Him God and Jesus. Yet this was not the name the Great I Am provided, but the names generated by man to deliver that makes you wonder why.

If the Father is not a man, why do people try and treat Him like one (Numbers 23:19)? Nor is He the son of man that He would make a mistake (Numbers 23:19). His Word is final, and it is Truth, it supersedes any fact or facts that have been introduced by men. If the church belongs to Him, why do men try their best to control it?

As it is recorded in Luke 12:16-21, it appears that the modern church may be too focused on building buildings. They gather people with preaching messages many want to hear, gaining wealth in exchange for their efforts. Their church is overflowing with wealth, but do they take the proceeds and refocus those gifts back to needy families, other churches, or social reform?

No, they rebuild a new church to hold even more people and continue to grow their own walls oblivious to what is going on around them. Is there a focus on The Father, the True Living Elohim, or is it set on church growth?

Conclusion

The body of Christ has always been the people. The church should have always been the people. When the buildings close and the religion fades, the True and Living Word should guide all believers into Truth, finally casting down the Facts. It will be as it was, Elohim's Truth Over the Fact that you may have been told you are worthless. You were raised a slave. You are a product of slavery.

Over the fact, the they's of the world tried to poison you by feeding you adverse chemicals. The genetically modified foods being consumed, drinks, beverages, and even your water is conditioned to harm you. To slow you down, dumb you down, and attempt to take away your connection with Him. Not to mention the invented technology designed to keep you a slave and vaccination programs prone to keep you sick.

The shots further weaken your ability to fight disease and potentially poison your body, mental state, and neurological functions, all in the name of national health mandates created by non-doctors.

The facts seem to point to a future that doesn't look much different than your past. Many would have you believe that your social, political, and financial status is designed to be always as it has been for these past 400 years until forever. (As if there was no pass that didn't include you living under the foot of another.) Likewise, some want the possibility that your past from times of old can simply be left on auto-repeat, and when this wave of hell is over, another will come.

You were brought up in poverty, and you will continue to live in poverty the they's pray. Only a few will make it out, instead of everyone leaving like it was in the times of Pharaoh. When the Lord told Moses to go get His people, He didn't ask for just the women and children to go and worship Him. He did not ask for only the men, and He certainly didn't ask for just the elderly. He did not care about the facts and circumstances around them.

He didn't care about the government the children of Israel lived in for some 200 years. He didn't care that the Pharaoh said "no," and he attempted to barter with the Almighty Yah! He didn't care that their skin colors were similar, and He was not persuaded, based on Pharoah's social position or the Egyptians, to change course. Moses had to be totally sold out and set on the Truth to ignore all the facts of imminent failure surrounding him.

He was not intimidated nor dumbfounded when they attempted to match His miracles with their witchcraft and magic. Moses did not repent when the Almighty sent the plagues and the final act of Yah claiming their firstborns. Moses did not change his course because they (the Egyptians) were losing the battle, and Yah did not repent for His actions. He, the Great I AM, is the same Elohim of old today (Malachi 3:6).

In Isaiah 55:11, it is written, "So shall my word be that goeth forth out of my mouth: it shall not return unto me void, but it shall accomplish that which I please, and it shall prosper in the thing whereto I sent it." The truth is that the Creator is in control, and His Word trumps every fact known on earth if and when He says it.

He can shut up the heavens so that it won't rain no matter the efforts of man. He can preserve bodies and keep them in good health even if they eat and drink poison. He is able to deliver anyone out of unspeakable circumstances and defend a people that would appear to have no God who loves and cares for them.

These so-called Africans have been treated as cockroaches in all nations, including the ones they were even born in. The conquerors would have them believe they are mere commodities. That they are an afterthought, a tolerable nuisance that The Great Creator made out of pity. That this same group was void of His existence, and had it not been for Colonizers and slavery, they might in fact, still be heathens. Journals of colonizers and slave traders, historians, and explorers would point to a different fact. These people were not void of knowing Yah but were forced to change His name or die.

I want to encourage you! This book was written to you and about you. The Great I Am has not forgotten about you but is and has fulfilled a promise about you. Yes, you have been brought low, but what great nations have not been reprimanded when they disobey and live contrary to the Father's Word or will? Who can stand against Him and live? No government, no law, no paper, no wind of doctrine, not fear, not turmoil, not guilt, not hurt, not pain, and certainly not anything wicked unless He permits it.

His permittance does not mean agreeance, for He gives His word that vengeance is His. He will repay the nations that have wronged the people of Abraham's seed as is promised in Genesis 15:13 and 14.

"13 And he said unto Abram, Know of a surety that thy seed shall be a stranger in a land that is not theirs, and shall serve them; and they shall afflict them four hundred years;

14 And also that nation, whom they shall serve, will I judge: and afterward shall they come out with great substance."

He spoke curses in Deuteronomy, and he promised bondage for 400 years in Genesis. He outlined the way they ought to live to receive the blessing and warned them about the curses. The good news is that the conclusion is not over yet, regardless of every fact that may point to the end. He said in Deuteronomy 30:1-3 powerful words that must come to pass no matter the facts of life today or the day this word would come to pass.

"And it shall come to pass, when all these things are come upon thee, the blessing and the curse, which I have set before thee, and thou shalt call them to mind among all the nations, whither the LORD thy Elohim hath driven thee,

2 And shalt return unto the LORD thy Elohim, and shalt obey His voice according to all that I command thee this day, thou and thy children, with all thine heart, and with all thy soul;

3 That then the LORD thy Elohim will turn thy captivity, and have compassion upon thee, and will return and gather thee from all the nations, whither the LORD thy Yahweh hath scattered thee."

Yes, He knew what would befall the continent of modern-day Africa. Yes, He knew what would happen to the blacks in the Caribbean, United States, Europe, Brazil, Angola, the Congo, Ethiopia, Nigeria, Columbia, Puerto Rico, Mexico, and all the nations that His natural children were spread. He knew that Hebrews would turn against their brother. He knew about the ones that would be a part of genocide and the slaughter of their own people. He knew about the ones that would sell His people into slavery without a care. He also knew about the nations that would come back and dominate those same nations.

The Father is not a coward, nor does He back away from His plans because Heaven and the Kingdom of Yah is not the place for cowardice (Revelation 21:8). Like what Daniel said, Job and the Messiah, I know of Your power, Your might and ability to deliver me, but if You choose not to and if I must drink this cup for Your Glory, I will still worship You. I will be a perfect bond-servant unto You and to You alone. I am willing to lay down my life because I know You will pick it up.

Through divine text and scripture, You wrote, those that try to keep their life will lose it, and those that lose it, trust you with it, will find it and won't be put to shame (Matthew 16:25, Luke 17:33, and Psalm 25:3). The Lord says vengeance is His. He will repay all those who have done something for Him in this life and the one to come (Deuteronomy 32:35, Romans 2:6, Romans 11:35, Matthew 29:19).

Deuteronomy 29:28-29 says, "And Yahweh rooted them out of their land in anger, and in wrath, and in great indignation, and cast them into another land, as it is this day. The secret things belong unto Yahweh our Elohim: but those things which are re-vealed belong unto us and to our children forever, that we may do all the words of this Torah."

It is our job as apostles, teachers, pastors, prophets, and those in helps to keep the Father's chil-dren informed about the Lord's promises, His Word, and Truth. We must be re-educated to have His Word and Truth at the center of our worship, not vain re-ligion. It is time out for charisma, and impress me church sermons, and time to get down to truth!

There is safety in following His Word and provision wherever He sends us. He is able to keep His children no matter what is ahead of them and behind them. Stay encouraged and feed your heart, soul, mind, and body the Word, and live it out in your life. To hear and not do gives you no benefit. You must be hearers and doers of the Word and the facts around you will never matter (James 1:22).

About The Author

"God blesses those who work for peace, for they will be called the children of God." Matthew 5:9

Krystal Lee is proud to have authored this book and accompanying course to better the lives of readers. She has a heart to help people in their deepest times of need. She writes because she believes there is power in sharing stories and life accounts, that others can benefit and learn from. Sharing is caring, so she shares stories, ideas, and resources to better the lives of her readers.

In addition, Dr. Lee has authored over 20 books across seven or more genres (adult, children, youth fiction, self-help, spiritual growth, novels, and more), in addition to ghostwriting and editing more than 15 published works. She has launched coaching programs, web courses, and helped in the formulation of many startup companies. Her specialty lies in aiding coaches, creatives, and service-based companies in defining their message, brand, unique selling point, client avatar, and generating a sales cycle and structure for her clients.

Empowering individuals is at the core of her work, and she is driven by her passion to continue writing. In addition to being an author, Krystal Lee is a business owner of multiple companies, a consultant, an ordained chaplain, and a speaker.

For more information about Dr. Krystal Lee or to engage with her further, please scan the provided QR code. To engage with the Coaching series and Monthly Meet up Group for Embrace Your Crown First Sundays at 4pm, please use the QR code or visit KLEembrace.com

Shop Books from AuthorKLee.com

Explore over seven different book genres, and find something suitable for every member of the family.

Scan to Shop All Titles by K. Lee

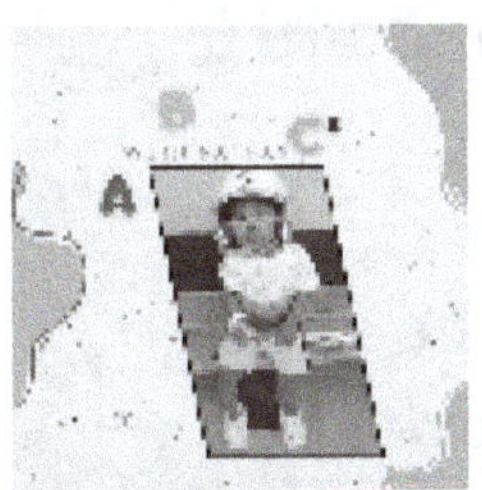

It's time to start and finish **YOUR Story**!

KLE Publishing specializes in helping people become authors. In as little as 15 to 90 days, we can help you develop your book and publish to 39,000 outlets!

Ghostwrite, Edit, Format, Publish
We can help from **Start to Finish.**

Scan and fill out the short form to learn more and connect with us.

KLEPub.com Authors

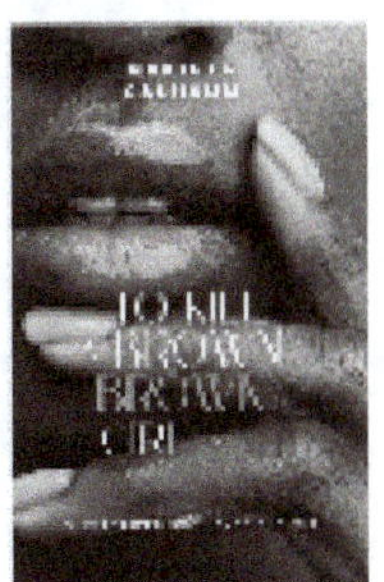

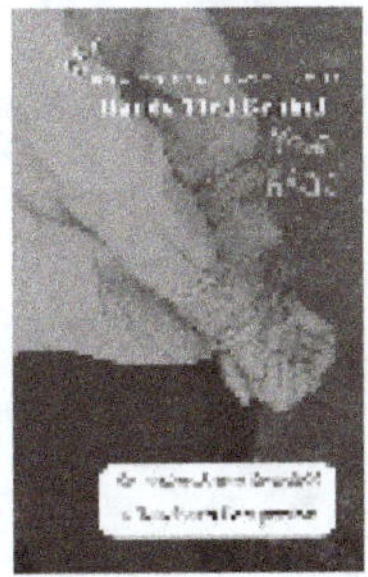

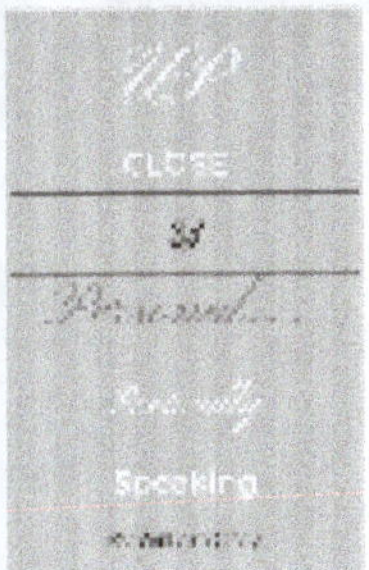